The LAST FIREHAWK

The Shadow Returns

by
Katrina Charman

SCHOLASTIC INC.

The LAST FIREHAWK

Read All the Books

1 The Ember Stone

2 The Crystal Caverns

3 The Whispering Oak

4 Lullaby Lake

5 The Shadowlands

6 The Battle for Perodia

7 The Cloud Kingdom

8 The Silver Swamp

9 The Golden Temple

10 The Secret Maze

11 The Underland

12 The Shadow Returns

scholastic.com/lastfirehawk

Table of Contents

For Brick, Piper, and Riley. And for Ethan Baskett. —KC

If you purchased this book without a cover, you should be aware that this book is stolen property. It was reported as "unsold and destroyed" to the publisher, and neither the author nor the publisher has received any payment for this "stripped book."

Text copyright © 2023 by Katrina Charman
Illustrations copyright © 2023 by Scholastic Inc.

All rights reserved. Published by Scholastic Inc., *Publishers since 1920.*
SCHOLASTIC, BRANCHES, and associated logos are trademarks and/or registered trademarks of Scholastic Inc.

The publisher does not have any control over and does not assume any responsibility for author or third-party websites or their content.

No part of this publication may be reproduced, stored in a retrieval system, or transmitted in any form or by any means, electronic, mechanical, photocopying, recording, or otherwise, without written permission of the publisher. For information regarding permission, write to Scholastic Inc., Attention: Permissions Department, 557 Broadway, New York, NY 10012.

This book is a work of fiction. Names, characters, places, and incidents are either the product of the author's imagination or are used fictitiously, and any resemblance to actual persons, living or dead, business establishments, events, or locales is entirely coincidental.

Library of Congress Cataloging-in-Publication Data

Names: Charman, Katrina, author. | Tondora, Judit, illustrator.
Title: The shadow returns / by Katrina Charman; illustrated by Judit Tondora.
Description: First edition. | New York: Branches/Scholastic Inc., 2023. |
Series: The last firehawk; 12 | Audience: Ages 6–8. | Audience: Grades 2–3. | Summary: Skull, the Shadow, and ten army rats broke into Perodia, and the other defenders must locate them and rescue the defenders' new friend, Bod, who is still trapped in the Underland with the rest of the rat army.
Identifiers: LCCN 2022013766 | ISBN 9781338832556 (paperback) |
ISBN 9781338832563 (library binding) Subjects: LCSH: Owls—Juvenile fiction. |
Squirrels—Juvenile fiction. | Animals, Mythical—Juvenile fiction. | Magic—Juvenile fiction. |
Labyrinths—Juvenile fiction. | Adventure stories. |
CYAC: Owls—Fiction. | Squirrels—Fiction. | Mythical animals—Fiction. |
Magic—Fiction. | Adventure and adventurers—Fiction. | Fantasy. | LCGFT: Animal fiction. |
Action and adventure fiction. | Fantasy fiction.
Classification: LCC PZ7.1.C495 Sg 2023 | DDC 823.92 [Fic]—dc23/eng/20220426
LC record available at https://lccn.loc.gov/2022013766

ISBN 978-1-338-83256-3 (hardcover) / ISBN 978-1-338-83255-6 (paperback)

10 9 8 7 6 5 4 3 2 1   23 24 25 26 27

Printed in China   62

First edition, November 2023
Illustrated by Judit Tondora
Edited by Rachel Matson
Book design by Jaime Lucero

⚬ INTRODUCTION ⚬

Tag, a small barn owl, and his friends

Skyla, a squirrel, and Blaze, a firehawk, are in the enchanted land of Perodia. When Talia, the leader of the firehawks, was kidnapped by a new enemy, Tag and his friends traveled underground to a place called the Underland to find her. Bod, an Owl of Valor in training, came with them.

There, in the dark world of the Underland, they found Talia. But they also found a new enemy: Skull, the evil king of the rats. Skull wants to take over Perodia and rule the land. He has an army of rats and Tag's old enemy, The Shadow, at his side.

With the help of Grey, the Owls of Valor, and Claw, Talia and Blaze closed the portal between the Underland and Perodia. But their new friend Bod was left behind in the Underland. And Skull, The Shadow, and ten rats from his army have broken into Perodia.

Will the friends be able to rescue Bod? And what is Skull planning now that he has brought The Shadow back to Perodia?

The adventure continues . . .

A SURPRISE VISITOR

A dark cloud twisted and curled in the sky above Valor Wood. Tag and Skyla watched lightning flash through the darkness.

"The Shadow made it through the portal!" Tag cried. "It's here in Valor Wood!"

Tag's heart raced as he swooped down from the branch of his tree. Skyla quickly followed, leaping through the branches.

TA-RAAA! TA-RAAA!

The Owls of Valor alarm sounded through the forest.

Tag landed in the center of camp with Skyla close behind. They joined Grey and Maximus.

Grey's eyes narrowed. "The Shadow must have entered into Perodia with Skull and his rats," he said.

"Owls of Valor! Prepare to attack!" Maximus ordered.

Tag and Skyla joined the Owls of Valor, and rushed to put on their armor and grab their weapons. When they were ready, they lined up in rows facing Maximus. They waited for his next command.

Tag's wing shook, but he held his dagger steady. Beside him, Skyla breathed hard, ready with her slingshot.

There was a sudden rustle in the trees behind them. Tag spun around, dagger raised.

"Tag! Skyla!" Blaze called.

Tag lowered his weapon, relieved.

Blaze hurried over with her mother Talia, the leader of the firehawks, and Claw.

"The Shadow has returned!" Claw said.

Blaze's head drooped. "Our portal failed," she said.

"No!" Talia said. "The portal worked. Most of Skull's army is trapped in the Underland. Skull and The Shadow can't fight us and win. There are too many of us."

Claw nodded.

Tag glanced around. Talia was right. There were many Owls of Valor, and there was no sign of Skull and his rat army.

Tag continued to watch The Shadow, but it didn't come any closer. Then it slowly disappeared into the clouds.

"Why did The Shadow disappear?" Skyla growled.

"I think that was a warning," Claw said.

Grey stood beside Tag, and he nodded.

"I fear Claw may be right. The Shadow is teasing us with the fight that is to come," Grey said. "Skull has only ten rats with him now, but we saw what The Shadow could do when it joined up with Thorn. With Skull's help, The Shadow can build a new army of spies here in  Perodia. We must warn our friends."

"I can help," Claw said.

"I need to return to the firehawks," Talia said. "Now that there is a permanent portal open between here and the Land of the Firehawks, they must be ready in case Skull or The Shadow attack."

Blaze looked at Tag and Skyla, then to Talia. "I will stay here with my friends," she said. "Tag and Skyla need me, and we still have to find a way to rescue Bod."

Talia smiled and hugged Blaze. "I am so proud of you!" she said.

Skyla turned to Tag. "What do you think The Shadow is planning?" she asked quietly.

Tag sighed. "I don't know. But whatever it is, it's nothing good."

THE SEARCH
FOR SKULL

Maximus and the Owls of Valor flew to
their guard posts, and Claw set off to warn
the creatures of Perodia. Tag, Skyla, and
Blaze stayed behind to rest for the night.
When they woke the next day, they went to
Grey's tree.

"How can we fight The Shadow?" Tag asked Grey.

Grey led the friends to his study. He pulled out a dusty scroll and unrolled it on the floor. The paper sparkled and a map of Perodia appeared.

"We need to know what Skull is planning," Grey said. "And where he and The Shadow are hiding out. We can't let them turn innocent creatures into an army of spies, like Thorn did."

Grey studied the map but frowned.

"What is it?" Blaze asked.

"This map should show us where Skull is hiding," Grey said. "But The Shadow's dark magic must be stronger than I thought. It's hiding them on this map. There is no sign of Skull or his rats anywhere."

"We'll find them," Skyla said.

Tag nodded. "We know Perodia better than anyone."

Grey gave them a small smile. "All right. But you must be very careful. If you do find them,

have Blaze send a signal to let us know where you are. We will come as soon as we can. Take the Ember Stone with you. It might help you," Grey said.

They gathered their things, and Tag collected the Ember Stone from its secret hiding spot. Then they flew out to the edge of Valor Wood, with Skyla on Blaze's back.

After a while, they landed in a clearing.

"If you were Skull," Tag said, "where would you hide?"

"Well, the Underland—where Skull and the rats came from—was a cold, dark place," Blaze said. "So maybe they would hide somewhere like that?"

"The Howling Caves?" Skyla suggested.

The Howling Caves were where Tag and Skyla had found Blaze's egg. It was also where Thorn's spies, the tiger bats, had hidden.

Tag shivered at the thought. "Good idea, Skyla," he said.

"Let's start there," Blaze said. "The caves aren't far from here."

The friends took to the sky again. As they landed at the Howling Caves, they heard the wind blowing through the dark caves.

WOOOOOOO! WOOOOOOOO!

Tag's feathers shook. "Is it just me, or has it gotten colder?" he asked.

Skyla's teeth chattered. "It's darker, too."

Tag took a deep breath as they stepped into the cave.

Blaze lit up her feathers to give them some warmth and light.

Their shadows danced along the walls as they walked. Blaze had to bend low, and her head brushed the roof of the cave.

Skyla pointed at the ground. "Look!"

Large paw prints were pressed into the dirt.

"Rat prints!" Skyla squeaked.

"Shh!" Tag cried. He heard a sound echo in the distance.

Blaze put out her flames. They waited and listened in the darkness, staying as still and quiet as they could.

Suddenly, a loud cackle echoed through the cave. Tag froze. He would recognize that evil laugh anywhere.

"Skull!" Tag whispered. "We've found him."

INTO THE CAVES

Tag, Skyla, and Blaze raced out of the cave and flew to the trees. Tag peeked out to make sure they hadn't been followed.

"I can't believe Skull's army is hiding in Valor Wood!" Skyla said.

"It must be so that they can spy on us!" Tag said.

"We need to warn Grey and the Owls of Valor," Blaze said.

Skyla nodded. "Blaze, can you use your firehawk power to send out a signal?"

Blaze lit up her feathers, and they shone orange and red and yellow. Then she flicked her wings and hundreds of tiny sparks shot up into the sky.
They glowed high above the caves, then slowly fell like fireworks.

"Grey will see our signal," Tag said.

"What should we do now?" Skyla asked.

Tag gripped his dagger. "We watch the caves and wait for backup."

The sun was slowly setting. There was no sign of The Shadow. And Skull and his rats were all still hidden inside the caves.

"Why haven't the rats attacked Valor Wood yet?" Tag asked.

"Maybe they know they are outnumbered," Blaze said. "Just like my mom said."

"Then we should attack now," Tag said. "We can capture Skull and trap The Shadow using the Ember Stone, like we did before!"

Skyla's tail twitched. "I think we should wait for Grey," Skyla said.

"The sooner we can capture Skull, the sooner we can go and rescue Bod from the Underland," Tag said.

"I do not think we can capture Skull without help," Skyla said.

Blaze nodded slowly. "Maybe we could go back into the caves and listen to what they are planning," she said.

Skyla sighed. "Okay," she said. "But if there's any sign of trouble, we get out of there."

Tag and Blaze nodded.

They crept back to the cave's entrance.

Tag felt around in his sack and pulled out the Ember Stone. "You should have this in case The Shadow attacks," he told Blaze.

Blaze took the Ember Stone. As she held it in her beak, the stone began to glow blue!

"I'm glad we have the stone's magic to protect us," Skyla said.

The light filled the entrance to the cave. But before the friends could take another step, a dark cloud surrounded them.

"It's The Shadow!" Skyla cried.

Tag reached for Skyla, but The Shadow blocked him. It separated the friends from one another.

"We're trapped!" Tag cried.

THE SHADOW

Tag could see nothing but darkness as The Shadow surrounded them. He held out his wing, trying to feel for Skyla or Blaze.

"Tag!" Skyla called out.

Suddenly, lights lit up the darkness. It was Blaze, shooting small fireballs! One shot past Tag's head, almost catching his feathers.

"Be careful, Blaze!" Tag shouted.

Skyla was trapped on the other side of the cave.

The Shadow swirled around the friends, pushing them farther and farther away from one another.

"We have to try to stay together," Tag called.

But it was no good. Every time he tried to reach Skyla or Blaze, The Shadow would push him away.

Then Tag had an idea.

"Blaze! Use the Ember Stone!" he shouted.

Blaze still held the Ember Stone in her beak. Tag could see it glowing faintly through The Shadow's cloud.

But then The Shadow pushed against Blaze, and she fell to the ground!

The Ember Stone flew from her wing and slid across the cave floor.

Tag dived to get to it, but The Shadow surrounded him! It was as dark as night, and Tag couldn't see anything.

He pushed against the darkness, but it was too strong. Tag slashed his dagger through the air, but it didn't hurt The Shadow.

I have to reach the Ember Stone! Tag thought. *Ordinary weapons don't work on The Shadow. I need magic. Powerful magic!*

"Skyla, Blaze, distract The Shadow!" Tag cried.

Tag crawled along the ground, searching. On the other side of the cave, he heard Skyla yell and shoot acorns at The Shadow. **Pop!** Tag heard the acorns bounce off the cave walls, but he felt The Shadow pull away from him and move toward Skyla.

Tag saw lights flash as Blaze used her fireballs. When the fireballs hit The Shadow, parts of it disappeared.

"It's working. Keep fighting!" Tag cried.

He looked around for the Ember Stone.

There! A small blue light glowed ahead of him.

Tag leaped forward. His feathers touched the stone. It felt cool on his wing. But then from out of the darkness came a huge, clawed paw.

Skull peered down at Tag. The rat king gave Tag a large, toothy grin, then snatched the Ember Stone.

NO WAY OUT

Skull laughed in Tag's face. His teeth dripped with slime, and his breath smelled like rotten vegetables.

"You walked right into our trap!" Skull cackled.

The Shadow backed off as Skull held up the Ember Stone, his red eyes glowing. "Now we have everything we need to create the biggest army Perodia has ever seen. We will destroy the Owls of Valor and take over all of Perodia!"

Tag leaped forward, trying to grab the stone. "No!" he cried. "I won't let that happen."

Skull laughed again. He held the Ember Stone high in the air, out of Tag's reach.

Tag held out his dagger and pointed it at Skull.

"Give it back!" Tag yelled, even though his wings shook.

Skull held out the Ember Stone, teasing Tag.

Just then, a brown blur flew at them from nowhere. It was Skyla! She scratched at Skull's face, and he yelled, dropping the Ember Stone.

Tag dived for the stone. He backed away from Skull and held the Ember Stone close, putting it into his sack.

The Shadow moved closer again, swirling around them.

Skull roared. His face was red with anger.

Skyla grabbed Tag's wing. "I hope Grey and the others arrive soon," she said.

There was a bright flash of light, and part of The Shadow disappeared as Blaze shot a fireball. She ran over to join them.

Tag looked around for a way out, but Skull and his rats had them surrounded.

The friends moved closer together. Tag and Skyla gripped their weapons, while Blaze held a flaming fireball in each wing.

Blaze shot out small fireballs at Skull and his rats. They backed up, afraid of the flames. The friends slowly crept toward the cave entrance.

But then Tag froze.

The Shadow's dark magic started to swirl around the rats. Slowly, the rats began to grow. They became taller and bigger. Their long, yellow teeth grew longer in their jaws. Their sharp claws curled like knives from their paws. Their eyes flashed orange as they closed in on Tag, Skyla, and Blaze.

HELP ARRIVES!

Skull peered down at Tag. He had already been larger than Tag, but now he was impossibly huge.

Skull pointed one long claw at Tag and jabbed him in the chest.

"Give me the Ember Stone," he snarled.

"Never!" Tag shouted, stepping back.

Blaze shot a fireball at Skull. He hissed and jumped back.

The Shadow circled the friends, trapping them again inside the dark cloud.

"What are we going to do, Tag?" Skyla whispered.

Tag held Skyla's paw with one wing and his sack tightly with the other.

TA-RAAAA! TA-RAAAA!

A horn sounded outside the cave.

"The Owls of Valor are here!" Tag cried.

Tag heard Maximus shouting orders outside the cave.

"You can't fight all of us!" Tag told Skull bravely.

But then Maximus's voice got quieter.

Skull smiled. "They can't help you if they don't know you are here," he said.

Tag's stomach dropped. The Shadow wasn't only trapping the three of them. It was also *hiding* them from Maximus and the Owls of Valor.

Tag glanced around. There was no way out of the cave.

The Ember Stone glowed blue inside his sack. If only Blaze could use the stone's magic.

Then he remembered—the Ember Stone had the power to create portals!

He glanced up at Blaze and nodded toward the sack. Blaze looked confused for a moment.

"Portal!" Tag whispered.

Blaze's eyes lit up, and she gave Tag a small nod.

"Okay!" Tag shouted to Skull. "I give up. I will give you the Ember Stone if you let me and my friends go."

Skull grinned. "I knew you would give it to us now that your owl friends aren't able to rescue you."

Skyla grabbed Tag's wing. "No! Tag, what are you doing?" she hissed.

"Skull is right," Tag said. "We can't win."

Skull laughed and his rats joined in. The horrible sound echoed through the cave. "Not so brave now, are you?" Skull said.

Skyla growled and shot an acorn at Skull's head with her slingshot.

He howled as he rubbed his head.

"Trust me," Tag whispered to Skyla.

Tag grabbed his friend's paw with one wing. With the other, he pulled the Ember Stone from the sack and began to hand it to Skull. But at the last second, he threw it to Blaze!

Blaze caught the stone in her beak, and her feathers lit up.

The ground began to shake. The Ember Stone glowed brighter and brighter until it was blinding. A dazzling hole appeared at Tag's feet.

"A portal!" Skyla gasped.

Blaze held out her huge wings and put them around Tag and Skyla.

"Jump!" she yelled.

Tag held on to his friends as tightly as he could and closed his eyes, wondering where the portal would take them.

Then the three of them jumped into the portal, leaving Skull and The Shadow behind.

DARKNESS IN THE STONE

T ag, Skyla, and Blaze landed on rough dirt. The portal closed behind them immediately.

Tag looked around, but all he could see was darkness. *Are we still inside The Shadow's cloud?* he wondered.

Blaze lit up her feathers and Tag gasped. He recognized the twisting tree roots and the damp smell in the air.

"We escaped Skull and The Shadow. And we're back in the Underland!" Skyla said.

"My magic must have taken us to the last place we visited," Blaze said.

Tag shuddered. The Underland was not a place he wanted to be. But then he realized . . .

"We can find Bod!" he cried.

Skyla grinned.

"Blaze, do you think you can open a portal again to get us out of here?" Tag asked.

Blaze nodded. "I think so. With the help of the Ember Stone."

She passed the stone over to Tag for him to put in his sack. Tag took the stone, but something was wrong.

The Ember Stone had been glowing blue ever since it filled up with the magic from the first firehawk's egg. But now, a darkness moved inside it.

"What's happening to it?" Skyla asked.

Tag looked around the Underland. There were no plants or trees. No sunlight. Everything was dead or dying.

"I think the stone is somehow being infected by the Underland," he said.

Skyla fell to her knees. "But if the Ember Stone's magic doesn't stay strong, we will never get back to Perodia," she cried.

"And we won't be able to defeat The Shadow!" Blaze added.

Tag looked at the Ember Stone again. Little by little, the darkness spread through the stone. The blue light began to fade.

"There must be a way to stop this darkness from filling the stone," Tag said. "Let's find Bod quickly and get home."

"Where do we start?" Skyla asked.

"The last place we saw him," Tag said. "Skull's lair."

Skyla's tail shivered. "Along with all the rats that got left behind."

Blaze stepped forward and then paused. "What's that?" she asked, peering through the trees.

Tag looked. For a moment he thought he saw a pair of shining eyes watching. But then he blinked, and they were gone.

"Be on the lookout," Tag warned. "We don't know what other creatures live here in the Underland."

THE TRAP

The friends made their way through the Underland. Blaze kept her feathers lit to help them see through the darkness.

Tag rubbed his wings together. "It's s-s-so cold!" he said.

Blaze held her wings over Tag and Skyla to warm them as they walked.

The path was covered with fallen branches and twisting tree roots.

"Do you think Bod is okay?" Skyla asked quietly.

"Bod is strong," Tag said. "If anyone can survive here, it is him."

Blaze stopped walking. "Do you hear that?" she asked.

Tag listened. The wind blew through the branches and dead leaves, making a rustling sound.

SQUELCH! Tag heard another noise.

Skyla pulled out her slingshot.

"Who's there?" Tag shouted.

Tree roots started to move behind them. Something large was headed right for them!

"Look!" Skyla shouted.

An oozing, glowing ball of slime slithered toward them. It guzzled up everything in its path. Leaves, rocks, roots were all swallowed into the ball of slime.

As it ate, the ball grew bigger and bigger.

Then the slime ball stopped as it came close to Tag and his friends. Tag's jaw dropped as two beady eyes grew on stalks from the top of the ball of slime.

"It's some kind of giant slug!" Skyla said.
The slug lifted its head and opened its wide mouth. The creature seemed to smile at them, then showed them rows upon rows of tiny, sharp teeth.

"It wants to eat us!" Tag shouted.

He started to fly, but his feathers were suddenly sticky and covered in slime. His wings were stuck! Thick, gloopy slime hung from the dead branches around him.

"Look out!" Tag called to Blaze and Skyla. But it was too late. They were stuck, too.

Skyla wriggled to get free, but the more she moved, the slimier she became.

"It's so sticky!" she moaned.

Suddenly, Blaze stopped trying to break free. "Oh no!" she cried.

The giant slug had caught up with them. It slid slowly toward the friends, leaving an icky slime trail behind it.

"I think we're in its trap!" Blaze said.

"Can you use your firepower to free us?" Skyla asked.

Blaze lit up her feathers, being careful not to burn Tag or Skyla. She shot a fireball right at the slug.

It gulped down the fireball, then let out a smoky burp.

"I think it liked the fireball!" Skyla cried.

The slug moved closer and closer, baring its sharp teeth. Tag tried to pull out his dagger, but his wing was too stuck in the slimy goo.

"It's going to swallow us up!" Skyla shouted.

ESCAPE!

Tag's eyes grew wide as the slug closed in.
Skyla screamed.

The scream gave Tag an idea. "Blaze, use
your firehawk cry!" he said.

Blaze nodded. "Cover your ears," she said.
She took a deep breath and—
SKRAAAAAAAAAAAA!

Blaze used her powerful firehawk cry.

The slug froze. Then it turned and oozed quickly away.

"That was close!" Tag said.

Blaze used her firepower to carefully burn away the sticky slime. It melted away, and the friends fell to the ground.

Skyla rubbed at her fur. "Ewww!" she said as slime dripped from her paws. "Disgusting!"

"We should get out of here before any other creatures try to eat us," Tag said.

The friends continued walking through the cold, dark Underland. The farther they went, the higher the twisting tree roots grew around them.

Tag used his dagger to cut away thorns and branches in the way.

"I'm hungry," Skyla grumbled, rubbing her tummy. "Do you have any food, Tag?"

Tag peered into his sack. The Ember Stone was now more black than blue. He pulled out a wingful of berries.

They ate the berries, but Tag still felt hungry. He was thirsty, too. But there were no streams or any signs of water anywhere.

"What's that?" Blaze said.

Tag peered ahead. A dim light glowed in the distance. It was as small as a firefly.

"Let's follow it!" Tag said. He ran off toward the light.

"Be careful!" Skyla called out. "It could be something dangerous."

The light came from a hole in the ground, dug beneath a huge fallen tree.

Blaze frowned. "What if it's the rats?" she asked.

"What if it's Bod?" Tag replied.

Tag crawled down into the hole, and Skyla and Blaze followed. It was just big enough for Blaze to fit through and it led to a larger tunnel.

They crept along the tunnel until it opened out onto a larger burrow. In the corner there was a nest made from brown leaves and thin branches. Tree roots broke through the burrow walls. And hanging from one of the branches was—

"Grey's lantern!" Skyla cried out.

"Bod must be here somewhere!" Tag
said, his feathers ruffled excitedly.

"Unless someone stole the lantern from
him . . ." Blaze said.

Tag froze as something long and sharp
pressed at his back.

"Don't move!" a low, deep voice growled
behind him.

OLD FRIENDS

Tag's wings shook as the sharp weapon pressed against his back. "We're looking for our friend Bod," he said.

He felt the weapon move away.

"Tag?" the voice whispered.

Tag turned around, his eyes wide. "Bod!" he cried, giving his lost friend a huge hug. "We were starting to think we'd never find you."

"I'm so happy to see you all!" Bod said. He laughed, then hugged Skyla and Blaze.

Skyla crinkled up her nose. Bod was covered in dirt and smelled very bad. But Skyla still smiled when she hugged him.

Tag's tummy growled loudly. "We ran out of food," he explained.

"Come in," Bod said. "I don't have much, but you can share my food."

He pointed to a wooden bowl filled with squirmy, wriggling insects.

Blaze gobbled up a few big grubs, while Tag took a centipede. He looked at its wiggly legs, then swallowed it quickly.

"I have some water, too," Bod said. He handed Tag a small cup filled with murky brown liquid.

Skyla picked up a wriggly worm from the bowl. "Have you been here all this time?" she asked.

Bod nodded. "After the portal closed, I tried to fight the rats that were left behind, but there were too many. I flew away from them. Without Skull to tell them what to do, they didn't chase me. I found this burrow and decided to hide out here. I've been spying on the rats to see what they will do next, so that I can report back to Maximus if . . . *when* . . . I get home."

"How did you find food and water?" Skyla asked.

"There isn't much here, so I've been collecting bugs and insects to eat," Bod said. "There is a small pond not far away filled with water. It's muddy, but it's better than nothing."

"I'm sorry we left you," Blaze said, lowering her head.

Tag sat down beside Bod. "We should have stayed with you, Bod. You saved us," he said.

"And you saved my mom," Blaze added.

Bod gave Tag a small smile. "You would have done the same for me," he said. "That's what being an Owl of Valor is all about. I've been training and watching so that I would be ready when you came back. You've come just in time, too."

"What do you mean?" Blaze asked.

Bod frowned. "The rats have been planning something here in the Underland," he told them. "At first they didn't know what to do with Skull and The Shadow gone. But then they started tunneling beneath their cavern."

"Where are they tunneling to?" Tag asked.

Bod lowered his head. "I think they have found another way to break through into Perodia," he said.

THE PLAN

"We can't let the rest of Skull's rats get into Perodia!" Tag said. "Skull wants to build an army to defeat the Owls of Valor!"

"The Shadow and Skull tried to steal the Ember Stone from us," Skyla told Bod.

"I've been trying to think of a way to stop the rats or see if I could find a way back to Perodia," Bod said. "Follow me. I'll show you the tunnel."

Together, they left the burrow.

Bod held the lantern and led them beneath some branches to a narrow path where it was easier to walk.

Then Bod stopped and pointed ahead. Rats were scurrying in and out of a large tunnel at the base of a hill.

"I snuck in when the rats were sleeping," Bod said. "There is a small opening between the Underland and Perodia. It started as just a crack, but they are digging to make it large enough to fit through."

Skyla gasped. "That's how the orange-eyed mole must have gotten to Valor Wood!" she said.

Bod nodded.

Tag watched as the rats went inside, then came out carrying mounds of dirt.

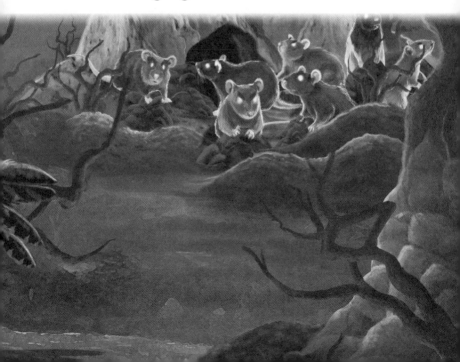

"There are hundreds of rats here," Tag whispered. "We can't let them get through to Perodia."

Bod looked at Tag's sack. "I thought maybe Blaze could use the Ember Stone to close the gap."

"That's a good idea, Bod. But . . ." Tag pulled out the Ember Stone and showed it to Bod. Bod's eyes grew wide as he saw the darkness swirling within it.

"We think the Underland is making the Ember Stone sick," Tag said. "I'm not sure it's going to be strong enough to help us now."

"But we *can* use Blaze's firepower to collapse the tunnel," Skyla said. "Bod, do the rats ever leave the hill?"

Bod nodded. "They go hunting for food together, and then sleep in the cavern for a while before returning. That's how I managed to sneak a look inside."

"Then we can wait until the rats have gone hunting, and Blaze can use her fireballs to destroy the hill!" Skyla said.

Tag grinned. "We can close the

crack so that the rats never reach Perodia!"

Blaze took the Ember Stone. "But if we can't use the Ember Stone, how are *we* going to get back to Perodia?" she asked.

THE TUNNEL

The friends hid among some tree stumps while they waited for the rats to go hunting.

"I hope we'll have enough time to destroy the tunnel," Tag said.

Bod nodded. "I think we will."

"I'll go and collect some stones for my slingshot," Skyla said. "Just in case we need to fight."

"We'll keep watch," Tag said.

Skyla nodded and hurried to collect stones.

Soon she joined the others, watching the cave entrance.

"Look!" Bod said.

A stream of rats came out of the tunnel in a blur of blacks and grays.

"The rats have left the hill," Bod said. "It's time to go."

They followed Bod back to the entrance of the tunnel the rats had made.

"Blaze, do you think you can destroy the tunnel?" Bod asked.

Blaze nodded.

"But what if the tunnel collapses and Blaze gets hurt?" Skyla asked.

Blaze smiled at Skyla. "I can shoot my fireballs a long way," she said. "I will stand up by the entrance and be safe."

"But how will we get home?" Bod asked.

"Let's close the hole first," Tag said. "Then we can find a way to Perodia."

"You three should stay back," Blaze said.

She lit up her feathers. Tag watched, amazed, as huge flames rose from her wings. Then the flames became giant balls. Tag could feel the heat coming from them. Then all at once, Blaze threw the fireballs into the tunnel walls.

Nothing happened. Blaze shot two more fireballs. Then the ground started to rumble. Dirt rained down from the tunnel walls.

"Get back!" Tag shouted.

Parts of the walls began to cave in as the tunnel collapsed.

"Blaze!" Skyla cried out.

Skyla ran to the tunnel before Tag could stop her.

BAM! A cloud of dust fell as the tunnel collapsed.

When the dirt cleared, there was no sign of Skyla or Blaze.

THE RATS RETURN!

Tag and Bod raced to the pile of mud and rubble on the ground.

"Skyla, Blaze!" Tag called.

The two owls dug through the dirt.

"There!" Bod said, pointing to a bright orange feather beneath the mud. They pulled Blaze free from the mud.

Tag spotted a patch of brown fur, and Blaze and Bod helped to pull Skyla free next. She coughed up dirt and brushed mud from her eyes.

"Are you okay?" Tag asked.

Skyla nodded, then looked to Blaze. "Blaze!" she cried. "You did it."

Blaze gave Skyla a hug.

Suddenly, there was the sound of footsteps in the distance. *Lots* of footsteps.

"The rats are coming!" Bod shouted. "They must have heard the explosion."

Tag pulled the Ember Stone from his sack. It was now mostly black, but there was still some blue magic swirling inside.

"Blaze, do you think you can still use the Ember Stone to get us out of here?" Tag asked as the footsteps got closer.

"I'm not sure," Blaze said.

"We have to try!" Skyla said. "The rats will be here soon!"

Blaze held the Ember Stone in her wing and frowned as she focused. Her feathers began to light up, but the Ember Stone remained dark.

"I don't think there's any magic left inside it," Blaze said.

The ground started to tremble as the rats neared.

"Try again!" Tag shouted.

Blaze focused as hard as she could.

Suddenly, there was a flash of blue light. It shot out of the Ember Stone!

Then Tag heard a loud **RIP** sound.

Tag looked at the Ember Stone. It was now completely black.

"Oh no!" Skyla said, pointing. "Is that Perodia?"

In front of them, through a huge opening in the air, they could see Valor Wood. Inside, Owls of Valor ran back and forth, collecting weapons.

"Is it a portal?" Bod asked.

Blaze shook her head. "It's a HOLE!" she said. "The Ember Stone has made a hole between the Underland and Perodia."

"This is terrible! Now the rats can escape into Perodia, and we have no way to close it!" Tag cried.

RESCUE

Tag glanced behind him. He could see the rats heading their way. "Quick!" he said.

He pulled Skyla, Bod, and Blaze with him through the hole. They stumbled into Perodia, where it was daytime.

Grey flew down from the sky and landed beside them. "What is going on?" he asked.

"Rats are coming from the Underland!" Tag cried. "We went there to rescue Bod, and we accidentally opened up a hole between lands!"

Tag pointed behind them at the hole. Inside, he could see the rats in the Underland running closer and closer.

The Owls of Valor rushed in and created a shoulder-to-shoulder wall, holding up their weapons.

There was a loud **SHRIEK!** Claw flew down and landed beside them. He raised his wings, and bright magic swirled around him. The rats on the other side paused. They seemed too scared to come through, with the Owls of Valor and the powerful Claw waiting for them. They turned and ran!

Tag sighed with relief.

Grey noticed Bod, and his eyes grew wide. "I'm glad to see you!" he said, patting Bod on the shoulder. Grey looked at Tag, Skyla, and Blaze. "And we've been searching everywhere for you three." Claw joined them.

"The Shadow and Skull trapped us in the Howling Caves," Tag said. "Blaze made a portal for us to escape, but it took us to the Underland."

"We found Bod in the Underland," Skyla said. "But he discovered that the rats had found a weak wall between our worlds, and they were digging a tunnel into Perodia. So Blaze closed up the tunnel."

Blaze lowered her head. "There was something wrong with the Ember Stone," she said. "When I used it to make a portal home, *that* happened." She pointed at the hole between Perodia and the Underland.

"Hmmm . . ." Grey said, eyeing the hole. "Well the good news is that after you disappeared, Skull and The Shadow went to hide out on Fire Island. The Shadow needs the Ember Stone to become stronger."

Grey looked at the hole. "But we can't let those rats come through," he said.

"Show me the stone," Claw said.

Tag gave him the Ember Stone.

"I think we may be able to fix its magic," Claw said. He looked to Grey and Blaze. "What if we all put a bit of our own magic into it?"

Grey and Blaze nodded.

"We have to try," Blaze said.

Tag watched as Grey, Blaze, and Claw joined wings. Each of them summoned their magic. The magic swirled around them in reds, blues, and greens. Then they shot the magic right at the Ember Stone.

Tag held his breath as he watched the Ember Stone. Slowly, a small light flickered inside. It glowed brighter and brighter until it was dazzling gold.

Blaze took the stone in her beak and stood before the hole. Then she closed her eyes as the magic began to flow toward the hole. It began to shrink, smaller and smaller, until . . . **POP!** The hole was gone!

"You did it!" Skyla cried, hugging Blaze.
Blaze looked to Grey and Claw. "We did it together," she said, smiling.

"We still need to find a way to defeat Skull and The Shadow," Grey said.

"How are we going to do that?" Bod asked, looking worried.

"We work together," Tag said. "The firehawks, Claw, the Owls of Valor, and us. We have to find a way to stop The Shadow once and for all."

ABOUT THE AUTHOR

KATRINA CHARMAN has wanted to be a children's book writer ever since she was eleven, when her teacher asked her class to write an epilogue to Roald Dahl's *Matilda*. Katrina's teacher thought her writing was good enough to send to Roald Dahl himself! Sadly, she never got a reply, but this experience ignited her love of reading and writing. Katrina lives in England with her husband and three children. The Last Firehawk is her first early chapter book series in the U.S.

ABOUT THE ILLUSTRATOR

JUDIT TONDORA was born in Hungary and now works from her countryside studio. Her illustrations are rooted in the traditional European style but also contain elements of American mainstream style. Her characters have a vivacious retro vibe placed right into the present day. She says, "I put the good old retro together with modern style to give charisma to my illustrations."

The LAST FIREHAWK
The Shadow Returns

Questions and Activities

1. Skull and The Shadow have entered Perodia. What is Skull's plan? What does he need to make this happen?

2. The Owls of Valor come to the rescue in the Howling Caves. But why are they unable to help?

3. Bod is reunited with his friends in the Underland. How do you think Bod feels when his friends arrive? Name three adjectives that you think describe Bod in this moment.

4. The Ember Stone was losing its magic. How do Blaze, Claw, and Grey work together to fix it?

5. Tag, Skyla, and Blaze meet a giant slug in the Underland! Draw your own picture of a giant slug. Then name your new creature!